OLD
HUSHWING

Author's Note

I learned that Old Hushwing was the country name for a barn owl when walking with Berlie at the Chestnut Centre, an owl and otter sanctuary near Chapel-en-le-Frith in Derbyshire. We knew then that one of us would write a story, and I got in first! *Old Hushwing* is, to the best of my knowledge, authentic. Barn owls screech at night rather than hooting. Although they sometimes hunt in the day, owls out in broad daylight may be mobbed by other birds. Female owls do tend to be bigger than their mates. And anyone converting a barn where an owl lives is required by law to create a new roost, as did Billy and his family. As always, the author is responsible for any shortcomings of his story.

AB

In memory of my mother

AR

Special thanks to Luca, Steve, Angela, Peter and Gary.
AR

This edition published in Picture Lions in Great Britain by HarperCollins Publishers Ltd 1999.
First published in hardback by HarperCollins Publishers Ltd 1998.

1 3 5 7 9 10 8 6 4 2
ISBN 0 00 664 649-2

Picture Lions is an imprint of the Children's Division, part of HarperCollins Publishers Ltd,
77–85 Fulham Palace Road, Hammersmith, London, W6 8JB

Text © Alan Brown 1998
Illustrations © Angelo Rinaldi 1998
Printed and bound in Singapore by Imago.

OLD HUSHWING

Alan Brown

illustrated by Angelo Rinaldi

PictureLions

An Imprint of HarperCollins*Publishers*

This is the story of Billy and Old Hushwing.

Billy lived with his parents in the Valley. The woods and fields of the Valley seemed the whole world to him.

In the field that belonged to Billy's house there was a barn. Mum and Dad never went into the barn, but it was Billy's favourite place.

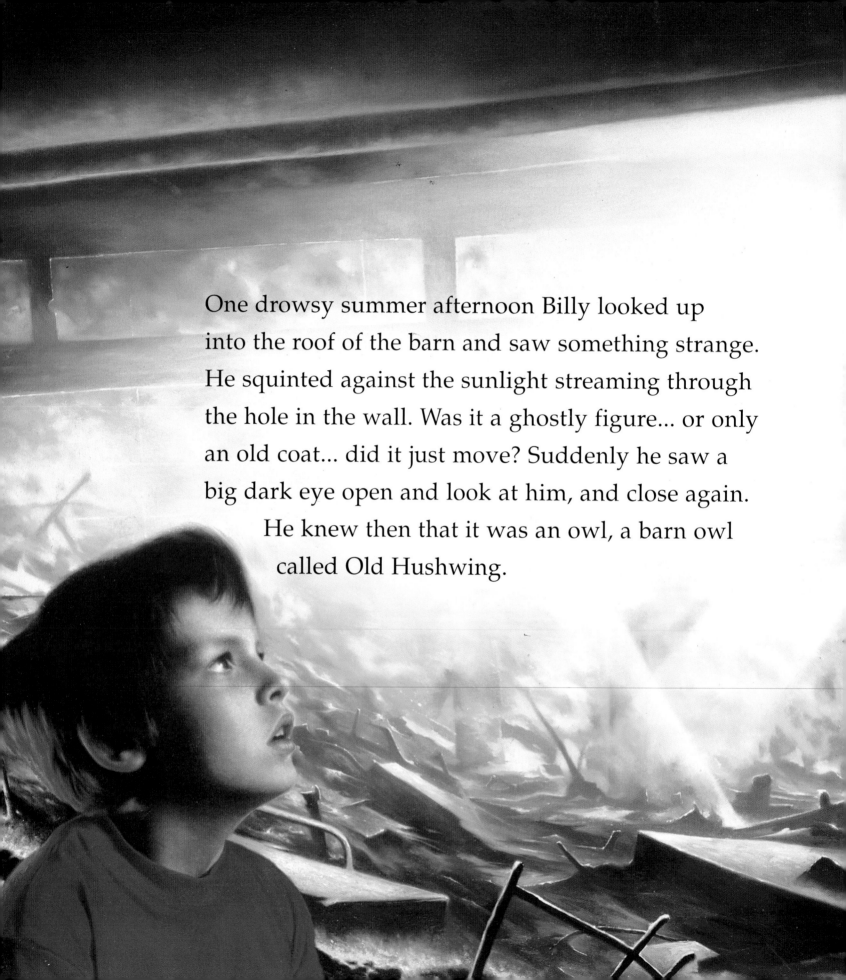

One drowsy summer afternoon Billy looked up
into the roof of the barn and saw something strange.
He squinted against the sunlight streaming through
the hole in the wall. Was it a ghostly figure... or only
an old coat... did it just move? Suddenly he saw a
big dark eye open and look at him, and close again.

He knew then that it was an owl, a barn owl
called Old Hushwing.

Every night Old Hushwing flew out through a hole high in the end wall of the barn, over the woods and across the fields. His flat, heart-shaped face and his downy belly were pale in the moonlight, and he flew in ghostly silence on soft feathered wings. That was how he got his name.

When Billy lay snug in his bed in the middle of the starry night, he often heard a screech, a lonely cry floating on the wind. It was Old Hushwing out hunting for his supper,

catching small animals in his great claws. But Billy never
told his parents about the owl in the barn because he wanted
Old Hushwing for his own.

Then one morning over breakfast, Mum said to him, "I'm going to have another baby, Billy. You're going to have a little brother or sister."

And Dad said, "We need more room for the baby, so we're going to get builders to make the barn into a bedroom – just for you. Will you like that?"

Billy was so excited he hardly knew what to say. It would be like a little house of his own. Right then it was the thing he wanted most in the world.

Very soon the builders came, but they had hardly started
work when there was a deafening screech and a tremendous
rushing flapping of wings. Chris the builder yelled in panic
and clung desperately to his ladder. Past his head flew
Old Hushwing, out of the barn, out of the hole high
in the wall of the barn, out over the woods,
and across the fields.

When the birds of the day saw Old Hushwing, they made
a great commotion. Crows and starlings, sparrows and gulls,
robins and blackbirds, they came down on Old Hushwing
in a cloud of feathers. They beat him with their wings and
stabbed at his big dark eyes with their sharp beaks.

Billy ran after them, shouting for the birds to leave
Old Hushwing alone, but more and more joined in and
chased Old Hushwing down the Valley and out of sight.

When Billy came back, Mum was giving Chris the builder
hot sweet tea in the kitchen.

"It was an owl," the builder said, "a fierce, wild thing."

"It was Old Hushwing," said Billy. "He lives in the barn.
You frightened him away and now the birds are attacking him."

"Well, what can we do about your Old Hushwing?" Dad asked.
"That barn is going to be a bedroom for you."

"Make a place for him too," said Billy. "Please!"

Chris the builder took another swig
of the hot sweet tea. "I'll see what
I can do," he said.

The builders laughed and whistled and sang and hammered and drilled, and at the bottom of the barn where stalls for gentle cows used to be they made a beautiful bedroom.

Then they sawed and banged and made the hay loft into a store for old suitcases and broken chairs and too small bicycles and all the unwanted presents that you must never, ever throw away.

Then they mixed cement and played pop music all day very loudly and made a little owl house. It was where the hole in the wall used to be, part of the thick stone wall of the barn. It was as big as a big toy box and it had a snug bed of peat and gravel on the bottom.

Billy called the barn Little House because it was a little house all of his own, and the place for Old Hushwing he called the Owl House.

But there wasn't an owl any more.

Billy lay awake listening in the middle of the starry night, snug in his bed in Little House, but he didn't hear Old Hushwing's screech as he hunted for his supper.

Whenever he looked, in the day or in the night, the Owl House was always empty. Billy was afraid for Old Hushwing, afraid that the birds had killed or blinded him.

It was cold fog dripping winter when Billy's sister Hannah was born. She was a little pink squealy thing, a bit like a pig, Billy thought. She was quite interesting, in a loud and smelly sort of way. Not as good as an owl, but not bad. And of course she had a room all to herself, though she didn't really need it.

There were so many things to do helping Mum that Billy
forgot about owls, though Old Hushwing still flew through
his dreams in ghostly silence on soft feathered wings.

Spring came so quietly it seemed at first that only the green sprouting trees had noticed. But then, suddenly, the air was full of life. Billy closed his eyes and held his face up to the bright sun.

Just for the fun of it, he climbed the scratchy snaggly tree in the garden.

When he got to the topmost branch, Billy looked into the Owl House. He thought he saw something strange. Was it a ghostly figure... or only an old coat... did it just move?

No, it was an owl. It was Old Hushwing, and next to Old Hushwing was another owl, a little bit bigger than him.

"Mr and Mrs Hushwing, living in The Owl House, Little House in the Valley," said Billy, very softly.

Old Hushwing turned his head
round and round towards Billy, opened
one big dark eye very wide, and winked.